Mary Blount Christian

SEBASTIAN
(Super Sleuth)
and the Impossible Crime

Illustrated by Lisa McCue

MACMILLAN PUBLISHING COMPANY
New York

MAXWELL MACMILLAN CANADA
Toronto

MAXWELL MACMILLAN INTERNATIONAL
New York   Oxford   Singapore   Sydney

Macmillan Publishing Company is part of
the Maxwell Communication Group of Companies.

Macmillan Publishing Company
866 Third Avenue
New York, NY 10022

Maxwell Macmillan Canada, Inc.
1200 Eglinton Avenue East
Suite 200
Don Mills, Ontario M3C 3N1

First edition
Printed in the United States of America

10 9 8 7 6 5 4 3 2 1

The text of this book is set in 12 point Primer.
The illustrations are rendered in scratchboard.

Library of Congress Cataloging-in-Publication Data
Christian, Mary Blount.
Sebastian (Super Sleuth) and the impossible crime / Mary Blount
Christian ; illustrated by Lisa McCue. — 1st ed.
p.   cm.
Summary: Clever canine cop Sebastian and his human John take on
the finding of an art masterpiece stolen in the very presence of
the chief of police.
ISBN 0-02-718435-8
[1. Dogs—Fiction. 2. Mystery and detective stories.]
I. McCue, Lisa, ill. II. Title.
PZ7.C4528Seb 1992   [Fic]—dc20   91-28633

To Ryan Scott Christian,
welcome to the world

Contents

1

Hint, Hint

Sebastian leaped onto the couch next to John Quincy Jones, his human, and leaned close to his ear, humming. *Ummmmmm, ummmmmm.*

John looked up from his newspaper, frowning. "Why are you whimpering, boy?"

Whimpering? Couldn't John tell the difference between whimpering and a fine rendition of "Happy Birthday to Me"?

A detective on the city police force, John should certainly be able to uncover this broad clue that his fuzzy buddy's birthday was almost here. But sometimes John was a little slow. And Sebastian (Super Sleuth), the clever canine, the hairy hawkshaw, the daring dog detective (unpaid and underappreciated as he was) had to solve the cases for his kindhearted but bumbling human.

Sebastian sighed. This was going to be tougher than he'd thought. He hummed again, this time more slowly. *Ummmmmm, ummmmmm.* After all, it was Monday night, and Wednesday would be his birthday.

John tossed his newspaper aside and grabbed Sebastian by the scruff of the neck. "You must have fleas, that's it."

Fleas! Oh, no, not the flea spray! It smelled like stinkweed. No wonder fleas wouldn't hang around it! And it stang! Sebastian's toenails scratched the linoleum as he pulled against John's grip.

Squeezing his eyes shut, Sebastian gritted his teeth and braced himself. In an instant the spray had saturated his thick coat and was dribbling down his skin, cold and stinging. *Achoo!* Yuck! How uncomfortable. How humiliating.

"There now," John said, patting Sebastian on the head, "isn't that better?"

Sebastian rushed back into the living room and rubbed his back on the carpet, throwing all four paws into the air and writhing, trying to get as much of the spray off as he could. *Arrrrrrg!*

John chuckled. "Such a silly dog. You're like a puppy!"

Sebastian rolled over and sprang to his feet, hope renewed. Puppy! Now they were getting somewhere. He bounded around the room, wiggling and

8

yipping. Puppy, birth, birthday! Would John make the connection?

John shook his head, laughing. "You'll never grow up." He dropped onto the couch and picked up his newspaper.

Then the phone rang and John reached over, punching the amplifier button.

"John!" It was Chief's gravelly voice. "I'm down here at the art museum and—just turn on Channel Two. Then get yourself over here on the double!" The line went dead.

"Channel Two?" John muttered as he turned on the TV.

The images flickered, then steadied, showing Amanda Chandler, Channel Two's nightlife reporter. "—repeat, we were at the Museum of Fine Art's reception of city dignitaries and art patrons for a preview showing of three masterpieces on special tour. One of these was only recently rediscovered.

"Suddenly the entire building went dark. When the lights were restored, the newly rediscovered masterpiece had vanished. Ironically, the chief of police was attending the invitation-only event along with other city officials, and he was standing no more than two feet from the painting when it was allegedly stolen."

"Oh, no!" John moaned. "How embarrassing."

The camera zoomed in on Chief. His face was so red it looked like a radish, and he was waving his arms wildly, shouting at two uniformed officers. The mayor was waving *her* arms and shouting at *him*.

"Chief," the reporter said, shoving a microphone toward him, "how could this happen with *you* here?"

Chief sputtered.

The reporter continued. "You personally set up the security for this show, didn't you? Two days ago you called it foolproof."

Chief curled his lip at the woman, then seemed to think better of it. He took a visible breath before answering. "The thief will not get away with it. My detectives will avenge this affront to the art world and to our city."

"You tell 'em, Chief!" John said, grinning.

"And they'll do it within forty-eight hours," Chief said.

"Forty-eight hours!" John echoed. "But—"

"Or I'll start looking for *new* detectives."

"Ohhhhh," John moaned.

Sebastian felt a twinge of fear. He and John could be unemployed, broke, homeless. Worse yet, they could be foodless!

The fear vanished as quickly as it had come. Sebastian licked John's hand reassuringly. The cleverest canine cop ever was on the case. He'd solve it.

Sebastian (Super Sleuth) was not ready for retirement.

2
The Impossible Crime

Sebastian paced back and forth, waiting for John to change into a suit. Finally John emerged from the bedroom and slipped his gold detective's shield into place.

"See you later, boy," John said, patting Sebastian on the head.

What did John mean, see you later? What good was only half of a detective team? Sebastian darted for the door with John.

"Stay!" John commanded sharply. He slipped out.

Sebastian glowered at the closed door. Well, he'd just wait until John was on his way, then he'd go. He pawed at the TV remote control.

"—is chaotic here at the art museum," the reporter said, "where we have just witnessed the theft of a Delavois that has only recently been uncovered. It had been missing since World War II, when it was allegedly stolen from a private collection in Paris by invading forces."

The camera moved about the room, showing two other paintings on the walls. A noisy group of men and women dressed in evening clothes milled about, talking to uniformed police officers.

"We are going to roll the tape again and let you see exactly what happened, as it happened," the reporter said.

Sebastian eased back on his haunches, watching. Maybe he could spot a clue.

The word *tape* appeared at the bottom of the screen as the mayor cut a red ribbon that stretched across the entrance to the room.

The crowd applauded, then moved past two police officers, one on either side of the entry. Sebastian recognized Officer Bridges and Officer Byers from his own precinct. The small room was a surprising change from the rest of the stark white museum. Red wallpaper with felt roses covered the walls. A fancy brocade love seat and matching chairs, along with a marble coffee table and a chandelier with crystal teardrops, helped make the room look eighteenth-century French. Three paintings that looked about thirty-six by forty-eight inches each were framed in gilded wood.

As the film rolled, Amanda Chandler told how Paris had been invaded during World War II and valuable art carried from the city, some of it hidden away in caves in the French countryside.

"Many works of art were stolen. Other pieces were hidden away by their owners. The intention was to bring the art from hiding after the war. But some paintings and sculptures were never recovered," she said. "There is much speculation about their where-abouts."

Amanda Chandler turned to a grim-looking man in a tuxedo. "Museum director Olen Hatchett is with me. When will the exhibit open to the public?" she asked.

"Tomorrow," he replied. "We're thrilled about all three paintings, but we're particularly excited to be the first in the United States to exhibit the lost Dela-vois. François Depaigne, the owner of the paintings, is accompanying them on the tour. Professor Raphael Diehl, the world's foremost Delavois ex-pert, had planned to examine the painting in At-lanta. But now he's decided to see it here instead and is en route at this very moment. Unfortunately, it seems that bad weather has delayed his flight. When he authenticates the painting, there will probably be a frenzy of bidding by art dealers. And it will all happen here!"

A little circle appeared on the screen around a

short, round man with more hair on his face than on
top of his head. Writing on the screen identified him
as François Depaigne.

"Herr Otto Stratmeyer, the exhibit designer, and

art patrons and collectors from all over the world are among our guests tonight," Mr. Hatchett continued as the circle surrounded a tall, wiry man with a shock of brown hair that looked like the bristles of a brush.

"It's quite a triumph for us to have this rare exhibit," Mr. Hatchett said. "Now if you'll excuse me. . . ." He snapped his fingers at a sour-faced man with a tray. "Keep the hors d'oeuvres coming!"

The man with the tray nodded, but when Hatchett had turned his attention elsewhere, the man scowled at his back.

"That was Olen Hatchett, director of the museum where this fantastic exhibit of newly found art is on display," Amanda Chandler said. As the camera moved through the crowd, she said, "We're looking now at Mrs. Lovee Lariope, who until this recent art discovery owned the most envied private collection in the art world. It's rumored that she has offered one hundred million to Monsieur Depaigne for the three paintings."

As the people crowded each other, struggling for the best view, the paintings were obscured from sight. "Let's make our way through the crowd and talk to Mrs. Lariope and Monsieur Depaigne—"

Suddenly the screen went black. There was a distinct, loud thud, a few gasps, and muffled screams and scuffling sounds.

16

"Don't panic! Everyone, remain calm!" Sebastian recognized the strong, clear voice of Officer Bridges.

The lights came back on, and the crowd of people were muttering among themselves. Mayor Cosley was on her hands and knees on the floor, looking stunned. Several of the men in the group rushed to pull her to her feet. Then someone shouted, "It's gone! The painting is gone!"

Officers Bridges and Byers blocked the entryway to the room. "Nobody leave!" Officer Byers shouted before turning to the camera. "Get that out of my face! Turn it off!"

"Not on your life, buster! This is news!" Ms. Chandler shouted.

The word *tape* was replaced by *live* as Amanda Chandler sighed. "That was the scene just thirty minutes ago, when the newly recovered Delavois was allegedly stolen. Except at the main entrance, the doors to the museum were all locked at the time, and guards were posted at the main entrance and in the hallway leading to the exhibit room. Ladies and gentlemen, we're faced with an art theft that couldn't have happened!"

Sebastian wiggled excitedly. Wow! A once-in-a-career opportunity to solve a locked-room mystery. And what an elite list of suspects! Some of the city's best-known people were there. Even international experts! The eyes of the world would be on this crime. Whoever solved it (and who but Sebastian himself?) would be a celebrity. Books, movies, television interviews!

John was definitely going to need his help with this case. But if the museum was sealed off to keep people from getting out, how was *he* going to get *in*?

3
Challenges Ahead

Sebastian skittered into the bedroom and nudged open John's closet door. He needed a disguise that would admit him to the museum.

The only people getting in now were police officers and detectives. Hmm, he thought as he spotted John's police uniform hanging there, pressed and inspection-clean although John hadn't worn it since he was promoted to detective.

Police would be going in and out. No one would suspect that the handsome officer was actually he, Sebastian (Super Sleuth), the undercover canine. It would be perfect.

Gently Sebastian tugged at one of the sleeves until the jacket slipped from the hanger. The billed cap on the closet shelf would be more difficult to get, but not impossible.

Sebastian trotted to the opposite wall of the bedroom and raced toward the open closet. Using the bed as a trampoline, he sprang toward the shelf, making himself momentarily airborne and knocking the cap to the floor.

When he'd wiggled into the uniform, he pushed through the doggie door. Then he pushed through the loose board in the fence and was free. He trotted toward the museum, reviewing what he knew so far. Three valuable paintings, one recently recovered after many years, at an invitation-only showing. The newly recovered painting disappears right before the guests' eyes.

Now, how could he form his list of suspects? First, by considering motive. Was it ransom, revenge, greed, pride, insurance? There were always plenty of people who thought they had good reason to turn criminal. But that didn't mean everyone with a potential motive *would* turn to crime. Besides, the room had been filled with the rich and powerful, not your usual list of suspects.

Next Sebastian considered opportunity. Who had been near the crime scene at the time of the theft? Usually that narrowed the list of suspects, but in this case it expanded it to perhaps fifty people, if you included the guests, the caterers, and the television people.

It was the third consideration that might help re-

duce the lineup of suspects—means, or method. Few people could figure out a way to actually steal a painting right under the eye of the camera. Was there a magician among them?

Motive, opportunity, and means—these were what a good detective looked for. Once every suspect who had these was on the list, the professional's job was to eliminate suspects one by one. No matter how improbable it seemed, the last remaining suspect was the likely criminal.

Although it was the fictional detective Sherlock Holmes who had established these guidelines for all good detectives to follow, he, Sebastian (Super Sleuth), found them thoroughly acceptable.

Everyone who had been in the exhibit room, including Chief, had had the opportunity to steal the painting. As for motive, Sebastian could only guess. Monsieur Depaigne, for example, already owned the paintings; his obvious motive would be to collect insurance, a possibility worth looking into.

Then there was Mrs. Lariope, who was rumored to have enough money to buy the whole museum. According to the TV reporter, she had tried to buy the paintings. Since Monsieur Depaigne hadn't sold them, her motive might be revenge.

The secret to uncovering the thief, Sebastian felt sure, was to discover the means. How could anyone get a painting that size out of the museum, with guards at every door?

If he did not know the guards on duty, he might have suspected that they'd been sloppy or had been bribed to look the other way. But not Bridges or Byers! They were completely trustworthy.

How, then? Through secret passages, like in those creepy old castles he'd read about? No, he reminded himself. The museum had been built only five years ago. Modern buildings didn't have such things. They did have air vents, sky lights, and chimneys, though. Fascinating!

The cautious canine skidded to a halt across the street from the museum, where he could observe without being observed. Blue-and-white squad cars, many of them with their emergency lights still flashing, surrounded the museum. Uniformed officers and plainclothes detectives, including John, were setting up the bright orange tape that warned citizens not to cross into a crime scene.

Several officers strolled toward the entrance, and Sebastian scampered across the street and fell into line with them. He stayed close enough to be considered by the guard at the door as part of the group, but far enough back so the officers wouldn't notice him.

The guard was Officer Pat Patterson, an old friend who always had a dog yummy tucked away in his pocket for Sebastian. Even if by some weird coincidence the thief had gotten the painting past Bridges and Byers, Officer Patterson would have stopped him or her. There had to be another answer.

Officer Patterson nodded as each of the officers stepped into the museum. Sebastian held his breath and bent his head slightly so that the bill of his cap obscured the guard's view of his face. He was waved through with the others.

Police officers were everywhere, poking behind statues, looking under hanging tapestries and massive paintings, flipping on lights, and checking doors for secured locks. However, most of the noise seemed to come from the east wing of the building.

Sebastian trotted purposefully in that direction. Suddenly, his keen ears picked up the familiar footsteps of his human coming up behind him. Quickly, the hairy hawkshaw ducked into an anteroom until John had passed. Then he hurried down the hall toward the noise, slowing only when he saw the shimmer of sequins and satin. People were gathered in small clusters in the hall, answering the investigators' questions or chatting among themselves. The bright camera lights—and the several cameras—were turned off, although the television people were still there, kept as witnesses, too, no doubt.

Chief was pacing and ranting. "How could this happen? We've never had anything like this happen before. Why now? Why me? I could've stayed home tonight, but no! I had to be here when it happened."

"How did all the lights go out at the same time,

Chief?" John asked. "Was it an accidental power failure, or sabotage?"

"The electrical fuse box is located in a hallway near the janitorial supply room. It was unlocked, and anyone could've gotten to it without being seen. Inside the box we found a timer and a device designed to shut off the lights briefly. It could've been there for days, or it might have been placed there tonight, no telling. The crime-lab boys are checking for fingerprints."

Sebastian doubted they'd find any. Anyone that clever would have used gloves to hide his prints, or at least would have wiped them off.

"Was every door checked and double-checked, Chief?" John asked.

"Of course they were checked and double-checked, Detective Jones. Triple-checked, even. This theft couldn't have happened."

John sighed. "But it did, Chief. Now let's go over this again. You say Bridges and Byers were at the only entrance to the room."

"Right."

"And Patterson was at the front entrance, the only door that was unlocked."

"Right."

"But by law all the exits open from the inside without a key or combination, Chief. Perhaps someone used a door without a guard."

Sebastian nodded. Yes, in case of fire, all exits in a building must be accessible to people. John's point was a good one.

Chief stopped pacing and frowned. "You think I don't know that? I know the law, John. But all other doors are marked for emergency use only. They're equipped with very loud alarms that go off when someone does try to use them."

Chief resumed pacing, slapping the palm of his hand with his fist. "The museum even added safeguards that hardly anyone knows about. Every item in this room has a small dot hidden on it. The dot contains a code that would set off alarms if anyone tried to take these things from the museum."

"The missing painting had the dot, too, Chief? Even though it wasn't a permanent museum display?"

"Yes. The dots don't harm the pieces, and they can be deactivated by a special machine. The museum director has that locked in his safe tonight."

"And you're sure you would've heard the alarms, even with all the noise and confusion at the reception?"

"Even then," Chief replied. "And just in case that did happen, I had cameras at the exits. They're motion-activated. The cameras would've gotten a picture of anyone walking near the doors. But I've checked the film. Nothing."

But wouldn't the alarm system and the cameras fail to work without electricity? Sebastian wondered.

"Chief," John said, voicing his partner's thoughts, "The alarms and cameras run on electricity, don't they?"

"The alarms and cameras run on batteries," Chief said. He made a growling sound deep in his throat, a warning that he was losing patience with John. "I've had them checked. None of them have been tampered with. You'll have to find better theories than that."

Sebastian felt sheepish.

John scratched his head thoughtfully. "I remember seeing this foreign movie one time where some guys came down through the skylight and—"

Chief threw up his hands in despair. "Do you see any skylight in that room, John?"

"No, sir, but what about the air-conditioning ducts. I once saw—"

"John!" Chief shouted. "Look at those air ducts! They aren't big enough for a person to get through alone, much less with a big piece of framed art. You watch too many movies, Detective Jones. Next thing I know you'll be suggesting that it was a trained monkey who stole the painting."

Sebastian sat back on his haunches. Oh, yes, he remembered that story. By Edgar Allan Poe, if he remembered correctly. He'd cut his teeth on Edgar

Allan Poe stories—literally—until John whacked him with a newspaper and took the book away. Of course, that had been when he was a puppy new to John's household. He'd had a lot to learn, he thought, chuckling to himself.

Suddenly Sebastian's back hairs stood up. "You there!" Chief was yelling in his direction.

Had he been found out?

4
Here a Suspect, There a Suspect

Sebastian all but belly-crawled to Chief, half expecting John's boss to call him a four-footed garbage disposal or a fleabag with feet, the way he usually did.

Instead Chief said, "Officer, you aren't going to find any clues on the floor with so many people tramping around here. Make yourself useful and get the floor plans to this building from the director's office."

It was a good idea. Sebastian padded across the floor, pausing only to suck in a few hors d'oeuvres from a side table in the hall. Chicken salad—not bad. But so little! It would take dozens of those pathetic things to equal one good-sized sandwich. Why were humans so intent on starving themselves at parties?

Sebastian found the rolled-up plans on the director's shiny oak desk. There was also a check marked *Insufficient Funds* in bright red print. The check had been made out to the museum and was for a one-thousand-dollar patron membership.

The check had been signed by Mrs. Lovee Lariope! If she didn't have one thousand dollars in the bank to cover it, how had she planned to pay for Monsieur Depaigne's paintings? And why did people think she was so rich? This could put her high on the list of suspects.

Of course, the bounced check could be a bank error. Sebastian noted that the check was from the same bank John used. He memorized the account number. Later he would call the bank's twenty-four-hour computer number, as he'd seen John do many times. That would let him know if this was a mistake, or if he needed to keep an eye on Mrs. Lariope.

Sebastian hurried to deliver the floor plans to Chief. Chief unrolled the plans and spread them out on a table in the hallway, using a small Grecian urn to hold down one side and an onyx jewelry box, circa 1200 B.C., to hold down the other.

Sebastian rose on his hind legs and looked over the layout. It was a maze of lines showing electrical wiring, plumbing, and air ducts snaking through walls.

Chief tapped the drawing. "Here's the exhibit

room, just as I said. Small ducts, no other doors, no way to get the painting out except by carrying it past Bridges and Byers. And no way to get out without being filmed except through Patterson at the front door. I want all three officers on suspension beginning right now!"

Humpt! Sebastian muttered. Patterson, Bridges, and Byers were good officers. Did Chief forget that the painting had to get past him, too? Why didn't he put himself on suspension! *Humpt!*

Chief scowled at Sebastian. "Did you say something?"

Sebastian looked away. He had no further comment. Yet he was sure that when all the facts were in, those three police officers would be proven as competent as ever.

Sebastian looked at the floor plan again. Chief's finger rested on the scene of the crime, just a fifteen-foot square box with one door. It didn't seem to hold a clue to who among the city's rich and influential was a thief.

Sebastian moved over to where John was talking to the mayor. "Ma'am, you say you were *knocked* to the floor when the lights went out?"

Mayor Cosley nodded. "Yes, a heavy object slammed me in the back, knocking me forward. I thought at first that someone was after me personally."

"A heavy object?" John repeated. "Not a person?"

The mayor shook her head. "No, I'm sure it was an object, solid and hard, like the side of a baseball bat."

John scratched his head. "I'm sure no one could've gotten in here with a baseball bat, ma'am."

Mayor Cosley shrugged. "I only know what I felt." She crossed her arms defensively. "We've got to solve this quickly. Our city will be the object of national ridicule. It's embarrassing to me politically and to our city. It'll cost millions in tourist dollars. We won't be able to attract exhibits in the future. We'll—"

"I understand, Mayor Cosley. We'll do our best," John promised.

Sebastian mentally crossed the mayor off his list of suspects. If the city was going to be laughed at, the mayor wouldn't get reelected. She'd be more motivated to make the exhibit a success than a failure.

Sebastian wandered among the guests, eavesdropping as they were interviewed. The Rathstones, frequent contributors to the museum and among the wealthier citizens and socialites, were talking to Detective Meyher.

"I was standing at the mayor's side as she spoke to the police chief. Right after the lights went out, I heard a sort of whoosh and thud. I was jostled, and when the lights came back on, the mayor was on the floor in front of me, and I saw immediately that the painting was gone," Mrs. Rathstone said.

Mr. Rathstone, who let his wife do most of the talking, nodded agreeably. Sebastian recalled that Mr. Rathstone was an electrical engineer. He would certainly know how to rig the fuse box to shut off the lights.

Sebastian sat back and scratched a flea behind his left ear. So much for flea spray. A whoosh and a thud? And he recalled hearing a thud on the videotape. Odd. At the time, he'd assumed it was a door slamming shut or perhaps hitting a wall. But there was only one entrance to the room and it had no door. So what had made the noise? The mayor hitting the floor? No, the floor was not wooden, and Mayor Cosley was a petite person; she wouldn't make that much noise falling. Had the thief dropped the painting? If so, wouldn't there be small fragments of frame on the tile floor? Yet Sebastian could find none. Perhaps Chief was right. Perhaps the tramping feet had hidden any clue that might have been there.

Sebastian's keen eyes searched the room, looking for something that might make a whoosh and thud. The only thing he saw that was even slightly out of place was a seam in the wallpaper that didn't match perfectly. It was nothing crucial, but certainly a surprise considering the reputation of Herr Stratmeyer, who was noted for his perfectionism.

Suddenly, down the hall, there was a terrible racket. It was coming from the front of the museum. A voice rose to crystal-shattering pitch. "I am Professor Raphael Diehl! I am expected here. What do you mean, I can't get into the museum?"

Sebastian peered down the hall as the man waved a telegram in the air. It was the expert who had flown in to authenticate the missing picture. Sebastian stared at the man, whose pale skin stretched so tightly across his skull that it looked as if it would tear.

"What do you mean, I can't get in?" he screamed at the guard who'd replaced Patterson. "I have a special invitation. I've waited in airports for a total of two hours, been on a plane for another two hours—all to see a painting that no one will let me see?"

When John had explained the course of events to Professor Diehl, the man said, "What a tragedy that a Delavois has been taken from us so soon after its recovery. Alas, there's little I can do now."

"Perhaps you can help," John said, "by telling us about the painting."

Professor Diehl shrugged. "I know everything about Delavois but virtually nothing about the newly discovered painting. I came to authenticate it, and to enjoy it—that is, if it is indeed genuine."

35

Sebastian narrowed his eyes, studying the professor. He said he'd only just arrived. But had he? Perhaps the super sleuth should check the airline's records to be sure the professor hadn't gotten in earlier than he had said, early enough to have stolen the painting.

John said, "Well, professor, we hope you'll be willing to remain here for a time. At least you'll be able to identify the painting after we've recovered it."

Sebastian liked the sound of that—*after*, not *if*, the painting was recovered.

"I shall certainly remain here until I'm fully paid for my services," Professor Diehl said. "Besides, the museum bought the cheapest nonrefundable plane ticket possible. I cannot leave until the schedule says."

Sebastian saw Monsieur Depaigne, the owner of the paintings, in an animated discussion with Mr. Hatchett, and he moved closer to listen. "I shall sue you for my loss," Depaigne said. "You promised me that my painting would be safe."

Mr. Hatchett looked as if someone had just hit him. "But the police are doing everything possible to find it."

"And you said the police were doing everything possible to *protect* the painting, too. But it is gone. I hold you responsible. The exhibit contract you signed holds you legally responsible."

"What will we do?" Mr. Hatchett said, wringing his hands when Monsieur Depaigne had walked away.

"You do have insurance, don't you?" John asked. "And surely Monsieur Depaigne has insurance, too."

Mr. Hatchett sank into a Louis XIV chair on display and buried his head in his hands. "We have insurance, but it is expensive because art thefts are on the rise. The deductible alone is enough to force us to sell our many assets. We might as well close our doors." He looked up suddenly. "If he sues us, we'll sue the city!" He looked happier. "Yes, we'll sue the city for breach of security."

Sebastian glanced at the clock on the wall. It was now four hours since the theft, and there had been no calls demanding ransom. Still, it was too early to rule out that possibility. He had the feeling, though, that there was another reason for the theft.

But what?

5

Means to Uncover

The witnesses were allowed to leave after they'd given their statements. Chief pulled his bow tie from his neck and said, "We've done all we can do tonight. Let the remaining witnesses go home. Us, too. We'll start again tomorrow morning. Bright and early, Detective Jones!" he said.

John yawned. "Maybe things will look clearer after some sleep."

Sebastian yawned, too. He could stand a bit of sleep himself, not to mention a midnight raid on the refrigerator. But he'd better get back home before John. It wouldn't do for his human to find him gone!

Sebastian spotted the guest book, which everyone had signed as they'd arrived. He glanced both ways to be sure no one was watching, then snapped it up. He would study it after John went to sleep. Maybe he would find a clue there.

Keeping his head low, he slipped past the guard at the front door and trotted down the sidewalk as if he were heading for a squad car. When he'd satisfied himself that no one was looking at him, Sebastian galloped toward home faster than any greyhound. He had to beat John!

He pushed through the doggie door and slid the guest book between the sofa cushions. Then he rushed into the bedroom and shook off the uniform in the corner of the closet. He could hear John's car pulling into the drive.

As John's key hit the keyhole and the doorknob rattled, Sebastian leaped onto the couch and stretched out as if he'd been sleeping all along.

John flipped on a light and Sebastian looked up, blinking and faking a yawn. John came over and patted his head. "Goodness, but you're breathing hard. Having a nightmare? Well, you don't know what nightmares are until you get a case like I have right now."

John flopped down onto the couch beside Sebastian and punched the button on the answering machine. Maude's voice came on. She was John's fiancée, and human of that spoiled Old English sheepdog, Lady Sharon.

"Hi, John. Sorry I missed you. It's a go! We'll be there. Love ya!"

We'll be where? Were Maude and her silly dog coming over again?

John grinned as he dialed. "Hi, Maude. Sorry to be so late calling, but—yeah, that's where I was, all right. How'd you know?"

Sebastian settled back, placing his head in John's lap, prepared for a long, boring bunch of sweet talk. Finally, John hung up and went into the bedroom. He made grumbling noises about finding his old uniform on the floor covered in dog hair, then went to bed.

When John was snoring softly, Sebastian pulled the guest book from its hiding place and studied its contents. Chief's name was sprawled boldly across the width of one line. And there was Mayor Cosley's carefully rounded signature, the almost illegible scribbling of François Depaigne, and the childlike perfection of Otto Stratmeyer's writing.

There were no surprises on the list. He hadn't expected to find much there, anyway. He had the feeling that the answer might be on the television tape. If only he could see it, and keep seeing it until— Suddenly Sebastian remembered that Channel Two was an all-night news station. He flipped on the set with the remote, turning the sound low.

When the museum theft story was repeated, Sebastian counted the seconds of the blackout. A thousand and one, a thousand and two . . . a thousand and five. Only five seconds.

No one could grab a framed painting, work his or

her way through a crowd of milling, confused people, pass two police officers, and get out of the room, let alone out of the building, in that time. It just couldn't have happened.

Yet it *had* happened. What had Mrs. Rathstone said? A whooshing sound, a jostle, and a thud?

The answer was in the means, but the means were as big a puzzle as the theft itself. The film was on again, and Sebastian turned up the sound a bit. Maybe he could hear what the mayor and the others were saying. Maybe the microphone had picked it up.

The camera angle didn't help a lot. It was aimed at the paintings over the heads of the guests. There now, that was better. A different angle. Of course! There had been two cameras at the museum. Somewhere there was tape of two angles covering the room. If he could just get into the television station, he might be able to get both tapes. Maybe something was there that he hadn't been seeing.

Thinking about clues made him hungry! Sebastian rummaged through the lower kitchen cabinets and found a box of crackers. They would have been better with some cheese, but the hungry detective couldn't be too choosy. He devoured the crackers and stuffed the telltale empty box into the garbage pail.

He cocked his head, listening. John was still

sleeping soundly. Quietly, Sebastian lifted the phone from its cradle. With a pencil held tightly between clenched teeth, he punched the number to the bank's computer. When he heard the signal given out by the on-line computer, he punched in the numbers of Mrs. Lariope's bank account. He waited for the next signal, then he punched in the number 1000. A synthesized voice said, "Approved for amount specified." Then the line went dead.

Obviously, the bounced check *had* been a bank error. Satisfied that he could remove Mrs. Lariope from his list of suspects, Sebastian returned the phone to its cradle.

He pushed through the doggie door. He was sure he could be back home, with clues to spare, by the time John got up.

What the four-on-the-floor detective needed was a new perspective, and that second camera might provide just the perspective he needed.

6
That's Show Biz

The television station would be open all night. And it was not that far from home—just a long dogtrot.

When Sebastian got there, he could see a receptionist in the middle of the lobby, at a desk facing the door. She, however, was turned away from the door, watching a television monitor. The program was not the Channel Two news, Sebastian noted, but one of those mushy movies on the dusk-to-dawn movie channel.

He nosed through the door and belly-crawled past her. There must be an editing room or perhaps a library of news outtakes, those parts of the film that were not used but were saved. It was probably somewhere near the engineers' control booth.

The hairy hawkshaw rose on his hind legs and peered through the glass partition. The engineer

had on earphones and was concentrating on his monitor, which showed the night anchor and the weatherwoman, with a weather map behind them.

Sebastian crept past the engineer and through the swinging door that said FILM LIBRARY/AUTHORIZED PERSONNEL ONLY. Now, how would the tapes be filed? He finally found them listed under UNSOLVED CRIMES, but it took him another hour to locate the tapes. Yes, there were two cassettes. Both were labeled MUSEUM DELAVOIS THEFT, with roman numbers I and II.

Sebastian pulled out the first one and shoved it into the VCR, keeping the volume low. Then he sat back and watched. This camera was shooting from the hallway. It showed the people as they arrived and milled around, eating hors d'oeuvres and greeting each other, and eventually moving into the room after the mayor cut the ribbon. While it provided a close look at each person who arrived, it didn't show much of the inside of the room.

When the screen was filled with nothing but snow, Sebastian removed it carefully and replaced it with the second cassette.

Ah, this was better. The camera was inside the room, giving a good view of the art on the wall. Monsieur Depaigne was speaking to Chief, although there was too much noise to hear what he was saying. He looked terribly nervous; he pulled a handkerchief from his pocket and dabbed at his forehead and neck, squinting at the camera.

He approached the camera, frowning. "Please do not put the hot lights near the painting. The heat will damage the work."

Was he really worried about the hot lights? Or was he trying to keep the camera from catching him in the act of stealing his own painting so that he could collect the insurance?

"We'll aim the light at the ceiling," someone off camera said. That was probably the camera technician.

"I would rather you turn off the light," Monsieur Depaigne said. But the technician ignored him.

In the background, Otto Stratmeyer was easing people away from the walls, straightening the shade on the lamp, rearranging a doily on the love seat, and plumping the pillows.

"Who's that?" one of the guests asked Monsieur Depaigne.

"Oh, that's Herr Stratmeyer. He designed this exhibit for my paintings. Since there were only three paintings in the collection, the museum felt the setting needed to be very special. They wanted it to look like a home in which the paintings would have hung in Delavois' own time. I'd heard of Herr Stratmeyer's work in theater stage design, and so I asked the museum to hire him."

Oh, yes. Sebastian remembered now. Herr Stratmeyer had won some sort of award for designing the sets for the play *The Disappearance of Markey Moore*. Hmm, had he designed *this* disappearance, too?

Amanda Chandler was standing just behind Monsieur Depaigne. "I've personally inspected the wallpaper, and there is not one seam that doesn't match perfectly," she said. "Exquisite! Herr Stratmeyer is indeed a perfectionist!"

Matching seams, indeed! Hadn't Sebastian remarked to himself earlier about a mismatched seam?

Herr Stratmeyer approached Monsieur Depaigne. "Did I hear my name called?" he asked, clicking his heels together as if he'd been called to attention.

"I was merely explaining how you designed this lovely setting," Monsieur Depaigne said.

"Ah, but you don't give yourself enough credit!" Herr Stratmeyer said. "I merely selected appropriate fabrics and wall coverings. It was you who—"

"Isn't that pillow on the love seat upside down, Herr Stratmeyer?" Monsieur Depaigne interrupted.

Herr Stratmeyer tugged at his tie and looked as if he'd just been struck. "Excuse me, please!" he said before scurrying over to the love seat to redo the pillow arrangement.

Such a perfectionist! He probably didn't own a pet. He'd never be able to tolerate shedding fur.

Mayor Cosley came up and shook hands with Monsieur Depaigne. "Good news, monsieur," she said. "The weather has cleared, and Raphael Diehl will be arriving soon."

"Oh?" Monsieur Depaigne said, glancing at his watch. "Soon, you say?" He dabbed at his forehead. "That is good news."

"Yes, he plans to do a chapter in his next book on how you recovered the lost Delavois and to do a complete critique of it. We are just thrilled that he has selected our fine city as his first encounter with your painting."

"Yes, indeed," Monsieur Depaigne said. "I look forward to meeting him." He dabbed at his face again before turning away from the camera and moving through the crowd toward Chief. The mayor followed, pausing to shake hands with some of the well-wishers as she went.

The crowd continued moving to and from the hors d'oeuvres table, chatting and laughing. They didn't seem to be paying too much attention to the paintings, actually.

Eventually the tape began to look familiar, and Sebastian knew they were getting close to the point at which the painting disappeared.

He watched as the screen turned black, then the lights came back on and everyone was flailing around, screaming.

Something was different, but Sebastian wasn't sure what it was. He backed up the tape to just before the blackout, letting it play through the blackout and beyond. The mayor was chatting. Chief was nodding and agreeing with whatever she was saying, as usual. Monsieur Depaigne was mopping and dabbing his face, and Herr Stratmeyer was edging closer to the crowd.

Everyone was right there, next to the wall, before the painting was taken, and afterward. If one of them took it, where did they hide it? And why didn't they feel someone leave with it? Was the picture frame the solid, hard thing, like the side of a baseball bat, that the mayor had mentioned?

Something about the group looked all wrong. He examined their faces. The mayor looked shocked. Monsieur Depaigne looked frightened. Herr Stratmeyer looked astonished, then placid. Was that because he'd pulled off the big coup, the big art robbery of his time?

Sebastian stared at Monsieur Depaigne. It was he who looked somehow different, but how? Sebastian backtracked the tape once more, staring at Depaigne, then forwarded it to when the lights came back on. His sleeve, the sleeve of his tuxedo, the one that was nearest the wall, was torn! He clutched the tear with his fingers, as if he were embarrassed to be seen with it.

Had it been ripped when the thief grabbed the painting? Sebastian didn't recall Monsieur Depaigne mentioning being touched in any way. Only the mayor had complained about being hit while the lights were out.

The cameras continued to roll. Sebastian saw Herr Stratmeyer draw Monsieur Depaigne aside, and the two of them went into an animated discussion. Monsieur Depaigne, in fact, looked pale and threatened, while Herr Stratmeyer looked like the cat who'd swallowed the canary. Did he know something?

Vigorously, Monsieur Depaigne shook his head. His face seemed to change color. Herr Stratmeyer smiled broadly.

"Hey, puppy! How did you get in here?"

It was the engineer.

7

A Rose Is a Rose
Is a Rose

Sebastian froze. He'd been discovered, and without a disguise! He decided that being cute would be the best defense. He sat up on his hind legs. He rolled over. He danced on his hind legs. He spun round and round. He did all the disgusting things that people like dogs to do.

It worked! The man started laughing. "If you want to break into show business, you'll have to find a different station," he said, scooping Sebastian into his arms and struggling under the wiggling weight. "We're an all-news station, I'm afraid, doggie. So don't call us; we'll call you!"

The man put Sebastian out on the street and

turned to chastise the receptionist who hadn't been attentive.

Oh, well, at least he had a lot to think about. He was sure now that one of the two—either Herr Stratmeyer or Monsieur Depaigne—knew more about the theft than he was admitting. But which? And how had the thief gotten the painting out? He knew the best thing to do was to return to the scene of the crime. Sebastian yawned. First thing in the morning.

Back home, Sebastian dreamed of floating felt roses. Such terrible wallpaper! He was glad to wake up in his plain and tasteful home.

While John dressed, Sebastian rummaged through the stack of magazines and catalogs that had arrived the week before. There, he'd found it—a dog supply catalog called *Dogalog*. If that didn't remind John that it was time to get him a birthday present, what would? He put the *Dogalog* on the dinette table, where John would have his coffee.

Then, holding a pencil between his teeth, he circled the next day on the wall calendar. Fortunately, it was Wednesday, John's day off, so he'd have plenty of time to spend with his furry companion—provided, that is, that they solved this crime right away.

John opened a can of dog food and heated some water for a cup of instant coffee. To Sebastian's dismay, John shoved the *Dogalog* aside without even noticing it. Disgusted, Sebastian gulped down his breakfast.

"Why you don't get stomachaches is beyond me," John said. "Slow down."

John dressed and grabbed his car keys. "You be a good doggie while I'm gone," John said. "I have to go to the library and research Delavois this morning. Fourteen hours are already gone, and Chief has publicly promised the answer in forty-eight, or he'll start firing detectives." John shook his head. "And I think I know who'll be the first to go, too!"

Sebastian licked John's hand tenderly. There were no answers at the library, but at least there John would be out of his way. Sebastian had the distinct feeling that the answer was back at the museum, the scene of the crime.

Olen Hatchett had insisted that the museum open as scheduled and that the remaining two paintings of the special exhibit be available to the public. He was probably right that it was safe to do so. There was nothing the police hadn't been over with a fine-tooth comb. Yet those keen canine eyes might be able to spot something significant.

Sebastian rummaged through John's closet but could find nothing that would make an appropriate disguise. Perhaps something would turn up on the way to the museum.

Sebastian trotted toward the museum, keeping to the side streets, where he was less likely to be mistaken for a stray dog. When he reached the museum, cars were already jammed into the parking lot. The publicity of the stolen art must have made everybody more curious about the exhibit.

As he strolled through the parking lot, he spotted a car with the windows down. Inside the car a wide-brimmed hat with a phony bird and flowers on it lay on the dashboard. A matching jacket hung over the seat back. He would take very good care of them, and he'd return them to their proper place.

Sebastian leaped through the window and wiggled into the jacket, which was fortunately a long one, long enough to cover even his stub of a tail. He nosed under the hat, then checked himself in the side view mirror. Perfect!

Confidently, he hurried through the front door and into the east wing, where the remaining two paintings were on exhibit. Museum guards were posted everywhere. A trail of children holding hands marched down the hall, giggling and mumbling.

"Shhhh," a tall woman cautioned them. "Remember, you are guests here. You must be quiet."

Sebastian figured they were a group of schoolchildren on a field trip. He fell into step behind them, since they were clearly heading for the special exhibit, too.

Sebastian strolled casually around the little room, thinking about what had happened. Five seconds of darkness, and a rare and expensive painting had disappeared completely. Byers and Bridges insisted that it hadn't passed by them. There were no openings in the square, fifteen-foot room that it could have been shoved through.

It was an impossible crime. It simply couldn't have happened. That had to be the answer. The crime hadn't happened. The picture hadn't been stolen. But then it was still here, right here in this little room, hidden, waiting for the right time to remove it.

Sebastian looked around the room. There weren't many places to hide a framed painting. Perhaps under the cushion of the love seat? Under the scarf thrown over the end table? He began to nose around, peeking in any spot, no matter how improbable it seemed.

"Look, Mama," a little girl of about eight said, "that lady has on a hat and jacket just like yours!"

Sebastian froze in his tracks. Would the woman recognize her clothing? Would he be exposed here, his secret uncovered?

There was a long silence before the woman answered in a raspy whisper, "I am so glad I decided not to wear mine, after all. It would've been terribly embarrassing."

Sebastian had exhausted all the hiding places—unless the painting had been hidden behind one of the remaining paintings. He tried to peer behind one of them. If only he could see better—

Oof! The wall wobbled as he rose and placed his front paws on it. The building was pretty shaky for one that had cost so much to put up.

Sebastian suddenly had an idea. He paced off the room. It was twelve-and-a-half square feet. But the floor plan had said the room was fifteen square feet. These were false walls! Of course! Why hadn't he thought of it before? The museum wouldn't have wanted its pristine white walls to be wallpapered over for a few weeks. It would have insisted on installing false fronts that could be removed without a trace and without damage to the original walls. And since this was a traveling exhibit, the viewer-ready walls could be set up anywhere.

The painting could easily be hidden behind the wall and carried out when the exhibit was over, along with the rest of the decor.

Sebastian's keen canine eyes searched the room, wall by wall. But there was no way someone could have gotten behind that false wall in the five seconds the lights were out. And everyone who'd been in the picture before the lights went out was there when the lights came back on.

A secret panel. That was it. It had to be. One of

these papered panels obviously slid aside or— What had the witnesses heard? A whooshing sound and a thud. That may have been the secret panel opening and closing.

Sebastian strolled casually over to the panel where the picture had hung the evening before. Slowly he scanned the eye-numbing red wallpaper, looking for a clue. Wait a minute! That panel where the painting had hung—that was where the seams in the wallpaper were not perfectly matched, where they were at least an eighth of an inch off. And where was the nail or hanger with which the painting had been attached to the wall?

Had it been wrenched out when the painting was snatched? Sebastian squinted slightly, searching the panel. There was no hole at all, not even a tiny one. This was *not* the panel the painting had hung on at all. But how had it been replaced, and in only five seconds?

Suddenly his eyes rested on the mismatched seams where one row of wallpaper was joined to the next. Sebastian rose on his hind legs and gave a mighty push.

Whoosh. Thud! The panel swung around on a central pivot and revealed the painting, still hanging exactly where it had hung all along.

"Look, Mama!" the little girl shouted. "The painting is back! I found the painting!"

Gasps rose around the room, accompanied by oohs and aahs. About that time, John walked into the room with Herr Stratmeyer and Monsieur Depaigne. All three looked astonished.

"That wall swung around, and there was the painting!" It was the little girl again.

Sebastian finally understood why Bridges and Byers had insisted that no one had passed them with the painting. At least now they—and Patterson—could get back to work, as they should.

And he understood why no alarms had gone off. The security system was perfect. It was just that the painting had never left the room.

"Wow!" John said. "Herr Stratmeyer, I think *you* are guilty of trying to steal the painting. Only *you* could have planned so far ahead to make such a panel. I think you planned on taking the painting out with the exhibit, then selling it, perhaps."

Sebastian knew that John had the wrong man. It was Depaigne, he thought, recalling the torn sleeve of his tuxedo. A few threads matching the tuxedo were caught on the painting's frame. But how was he going to let John know?

"No, no!" Herr Stratmeyer shouted. "I only followed the designs given me by François Depaigne. The swinging panel was his idea! I had nothing to do with the theft! I didn't know why he wanted such a design until after the painting disappeared."

"You idiot!" Monsieur Depaigne said. "You were quick enough to try to blackmail me when you did know!"

Words tumbled from their mouths like marbles from a sack as each tried to blame the other. Soon they revealed that the painting was actually a fake. The forger, posing as an art dealer, had duped Monsieur Depaigne into buying it. When Depaigne discovered that the painting was a fake, he determined to recoup his money, either by selling the painting to an unsuspecting art collector, or by faking a theft and getting the insurance companies and the museum to pay for it. What would it matter if the painting was never recovered? He would have his money, and no one would be the wiser.

But when he discovered that Professor Diehl was due at any moment, he knew the painting would be discredited.

"Monsieur Depaigne had me make all of the panels double sided and on pivots," Herr Stratmeyer explained. "He said it was in case one side was damaged or became too dirty. I swear!"

"I think we will let the courts figure out how to spread the guilt," John said as he reached into his pocket for handcuffs. He pulled out the small white card he kept in his shirt pocket and read the two men their rights. "But how did the picture reappear?" he said.

The little girl, who'd been watching the activities with wonder-wide eyes, pointed at Sebastian. "That lady in the hat fell against the wall, and it swung around, that's how."

Sebastian pushed past John and the two men and dashed down the hall toward the door. Fell, indeed! Didn't that girl recognize good detective work when she saw it?

"Hey, lady! Wait!" John shouted. "Come back, lady! Don't you want the reward the museum has offered?"

Solving a case was reward enough, the hairy hawkshaw thought as he raced toward the car to deposit the borrowed clothes. And he'd done it in only sixteen hours! When Sebastian (Super Sleuth) was on the job, there was no need for all that extra time, he thought smugly. Then he trotted home, satisfied.

When John arrived later, he headed straight for the kitchen. "Hey, good buddy," he called to Sebastian, "it's all over. Thank goodness! I was worried that I wouldn't be able to solve this case in time to bake your birthday cake.

"You probably don't know it, but tomorrow's your birthday. And Maude and Lady Sharon are coming over tonight to help celebrate."

Sebastian sighed contentedly. *He'd* solved the crime but John had remembered his birthday. He wouldn't even mind sharing it with Maude and Lady Sharon.

Softly he hummed to himself. Hap-py birth-day toooo meeee. *Ummmmmm.*

"You sound as if you're bothered by fleas again," John said.

Sebastian sighed. It was a dog's life. But it wasn't all bad, even if it did include flea spray!